Holly

This series is for my riding friend Shelley,
who cares about all animals.

Visit the Animal Magic website:
www.animalmagicrescue.net

STRIPES PUBLISHING
An imprint of Magi Publications
1 The Coda Centre, 189 Munster Road, London SW6 6AW

A paperback original
First published in Great Britain in 2008

ISBN: 978-1-84715-063-9

Printed and bound in Belgium

2 4 6 8 10 9 7 5 3 1

Holly

Tina Nolan
Illustrated by Sharon Rentta

 HOME   ADOPT    FRIENDS

ANIMAL MAGIC
Meet the animals

Visit our website at
www.animalmagicrescue.net

Working our
magic to match
the perfect pet
with the perfect
owner!

LOTTIE
Lottie would love a warm
home and family of her
own. Can you give her the
care she needs?

BUFFY
Buffy is a lap cat. Curl up
for lots of cosy nights with
this gorgeous girl –
purrfect!

FLASH
A sweet cat with big paws!
Flash loves the outdoors.
He needs a big garden
away from main roads.

RESCUE CENTRE
in need of a home!

SASHA AND RUBY

Two fluffy youngsters who
need a home together.
Are you willing to comb
and cuddle them?

CHARLIE

A lively boy, good with
children. Recovering from
an operation, so needs
plenty of TLC.

BRUNO

Don't let his tough act
fool you – Bruno's a shy,
retiring type who will
follow wherever you go.

MAX

Max's elderly owner has
been taken into hospital.
Can you give him a
new home?

Chapter One

"Karl, come and look at this!" On the Monday before Christmas, Eva Harrison called her brother into the yard at Animal Magic Rescue Centre.

Karl stuck his head out of the stable block. "I can't right now. I've got to finish mucking out Rosie's stable."

"It won't take a minute. Just come and look at this puppy playing with the yard brush." Eva couldn't help laughing. The tiny black and white Border collie had clamped her jaws on to the bristles and was growling and tugging the whole thing into the middle of the frosty yard. "She thinks she's really fierce!"

"Yap!" The pup wriggled and rolled, covering herself in white frost and almost whacking herself with the broom handle.

Though he was busy mucking out, Karl came to have a look. "Who does she belong to?"

"Mr Price brought her in with three other puppies. Mum has given them their first set of injections. This one made a run for it. You're an escapee, aren't you?" Eva said, crouching down and stroking the pup. "But you're very, very cute."

"Not bad," Karl said, picking the puppy up and dusting her down. "We can find a home for you, no problem. And your brothers and sisters, too."

The lively pup licked Karl's hand and wriggled free. Once more she stalked the yard brush, then pounced. "Yip-yap-yap!"

"Gorgeous!" Eva sighed. It was one of her dreams to have a puppy of her own, but her mum and dad had a strict rule about not adopting any of the pets who came into the centre.

"Come back here, you little monkey!" a voice called from the doorway into Reception. It was the puppy's owner, Joe Price, who lived up at Moorview Farm.

At last Eva persuaded the puppy to let go of the brush. She carried her across to the farmer. "What's her name?" Eva asked, handing the pup over.

"This one is called Holly." The farmer half smiled as he grasped the wriggling puppy. "There's one other bitch in the litter. She's called Ivy. Holly and Ivy – Christmas puppies, get it?" A proper grin spread across his face. "The dogs are Bill and Ben."

"Holly, Ivy, Bill and Ben." Karl repeated the names. "Would you like us to put them on the Animal Magic website?"

Joe Price shook his head. "No need for that. I'm hoping to turn three of these pups into working dogs. Bill is going to Adam Ingleby over at High Trees."

"We know Adam," Eva broke in. "He helped us set up a hedgehog sanctuary in the woods behind the farm."

The farmer nodded in response. "Ivy will stay with me and Ben is going to my cousin's sheep farm up north. He has a farm near Gretna, and is planning to train Ben for top level sheepdog trials."

Eva and Karl followed Joe back into Reception where their mum, Heidi, and vet's assistant Jen were entering the pups' details on to the computer.

"And what about Holly?" Eva smiled wistfully as her favourite of the four pups refused to go back into Joe's well-used pet carrier.

"Yip!" Holly cried, climbing out of the carrier and launching herself from the desk on to the floor.

Karl lunged at her, but Holly was too quick. She scooted under the magazine rack and hid under the bench in the waiting area.

"She's a livewire, this one," Joe chuckled. "And she's probably the brightest of the bunch. But she's not going to be put to work. I've sold her to a woman who stopped at the farm the other day to buy a Christmas holly wreath. Her name's Andrea Waterson. She lives somewhere in town. To be honest, I don't know much more than that about her." Joe looked at his watch and realized he had to go. "Holly's clever, so I hope the Watersons take her to dog-training classes – otherwise she could be quite a handful!"

While Karl went after Holly, Eva fired questions at the farmer. "Have you told Mrs Waterson about training Holly properly? Does she have a nice big garden? Does she realize that dogs need at least two good walks a day?"

"Whooaa!" Joe begged, grinning at

Heidi Harrison and holding up his hands in mock surrender.

"Sorry about my daughter giving you the third degree, Joe," Heidi broke in with an apologetic smile. "Eva worries about every creature in the entire world!"

Mr Price nodded. "I must admit, I wasn't that happy about selling Holly to Mrs Waterson," he muttered. "But she offered me a good price and I accepted."

"I know, Joe. Times are hard for farmers these days," Heidi sympathized. "You have to earn money where you can."

"Come on, let's get you back into the carrier," Karl said to Holly as he cornered her under the bench and picked her up. This time Holly didn't struggle as he stroked her then snuggled her in beside her sister and brothers.

"Remind me – are the puppies fully weaned?" Jen asked Joe for her records.

"Yes. They're eight weeks old and their mum's just about had enough of them," Joe replied. "They're on solid food three times a day."

"And we've given you wormers for them, plus they've had their anti-flea treatment along with everything else." Jen saved the updated file before closing the screen. "That's everything then. They're ready to face the big wide world. I can print out vaccination certificates and send them to you in the next couple of days."

"Great. That means I can let the new owners know that they can collect them before Christmas." The farmer closed the carrier and picked it up. The puppies yapped and scrabbled inside.

"Good luck!" Heidi called after him, raising her eyebrows at Eva as Joe crossed the frosty yard. "Don't even think about it!"

"What?" Eva faked ignorance.

"I know you, Eva! Don't think about running after Joe and quizzing him again about Holly's new owner!"

"B-b-but...!" Eva hadn't liked the sound of Mrs Waterson – the woman who'd gone to Moorview to buy a holly wreath, but ended up walking away with a puppy as well. "What if she doesn't know anything about how to look after a dog?"

"Your worries might well be justified," Heidi said firmly, watching the farmer put the pet carrier into his Land Rover and drive off. "But it's none of our business, Eva. There isn't a thing we can do."

Chapter Two

As Joe Price drove out of Animal Magic with his four adorable pups, Eva and Karl's dad drove in. He jumped out of his delivery van and ran round to the back doors. "Can you give me a hand with this cat?" he yelled. "Watch you don't slip on the ice!"

"Go and fetch a carrier," Heidi told Karl, as she and Eva rushed over to the van.

"I'm sure she's a stray. I found her on the allotments at the back of the parcel depot," Mark Harrison explained as he eased open the door. "They're pretty much deserted at this time of year – no one's out there digging when the ground's frozen. The poor creature had been forced to make a den under one of the sheds. I expect she'd have frozen to death if she'd stayed out much longer."

Heidi nodded. "They're forecasting minus five degrees tonight. And I doubt she'll have eaten lately either."

"Poor thing!" Eva cried as her mum reached in and took hold of the stray.

The female cat was a mixture of brown, black and dirty white. Hardly more than skin and bone, she looked as if she'd given in and was ready to die.

Karl reappeared with the carrier and Heidi gently lowered the patient in and rushed back to the surgery.

"Eva, fetch a blanket to wrap her in," Heidi ordered. "We need to restore her body temperature and rehydrate her as quickly as we can. Jen, we'll need to hook her up to a drip." Quickly, Heidi took control, fighting to save the cat, who lay on her side without moving. "Somebody give her a name," she suggested.

"Lottie!" The name came to Eva straight away. "Because she was found on an allotment."

"OK, Lottie, you'll feel a small prick," Heidi said gently as she inserted the needle to connect her to the drip. "Jen and I are going to take you next door into the cattery and put you under a nice heat lamp. When you're feeling better, we'll give you a more thorough examination."

The cat blinked and took a deep breath. She didn't raise her head as she was carried next door.

"I'll start on her website entry," Karl decided, typing some words into a Drafts file. "Lottie would love a warm home and a family of her own. Can you give her the care she needs?"

"Yes, that's good. But don't put it up on the site yet," Heidi advised.

"I feel so sorry for her," Eva murmured. "Let's just hope that Dad found her in time." Then she remembered something. "Hey, Karl, did you close the stable door when you came out to see Holly?"

"Uh-oh! I don't think I did."

Karl and Eva dashed out into the yard, just in time to see Rosie taking advantage of the open door. The shaggy little Shetland pony ventured out into the yard, closely followed by cheeky Merlin.

"Stop!" Eva cried, waving her arms and trying to shoo Rosie and Merlin back the way they'd come.

The Shetland and the grey foal slid and skidded on the icy surface while Merlin's mother, Guinevere, stuck her head over the stable door and whinnied.

"That's right, Gwinnie – you tell them to stop messing about!" Eva muttered, grabbing Rosie's head collar and turning her round. "Uh-oh, here comes Annie!"

Sure enough, her neighbour, Annie Brooks, had been out in her drive and had heard the clatter of hooves. She and her mum were boarding Guinevere, Merlin and Rosie at Animal Magic until their new stables were finished. "What's going on?" she asked.

"Nothing. It's OK. Karl and I were just about to take these three out into the field to save you the bother." Eva tried to make it sound as if everything was under control, but naughty Rosie was making it difficult.

"They'll need their rugs," Annie decided, fetching them from the tack room. "Mum and Dad are out in the field. Dad's taken time off work to finish building the stables. He says they should be ready by Christmas. Mum wants to have a party to celebrate – maybe at New Year."

"Cool!" Quickly Eva and Annie put on Rosie and Merlin's winter rugs while Karl fastened a halter on Guinevere. Soon they were all on their way to the Brookses' field.

"Hey, Gwinnie, look at that!" Karl exclaimed when he saw Annie's parents hard at work on the wooden stables. "That's five star accommodation for horses!"

Jason Brooks looked up from his hammering. "Hi there!" he called.

"They look amazing," Eva said, letting Rosie go and walking up the hill to inspect the stable block. "The horses are going to love it!"

"And you and Karl will no doubt be glad not to have to muck them out at

your place." Linda handed Jason another handful of nails then stood back to admire their work. "They'll be off your hands for good."

"We've loved having them to stay," Eva protested. "We're going to miss them."

"Well, feel free to come and muck out here as often as you like!" Mr Brooks grinned. "And tell your grandad to take as much manure as he likes for the plants at his garden centre!"

"Will do!" Eva grinned. It was time to go. There was still a heap of stuff to do, including checking on Lottie and putting up a Christmas tree. "Better go!" she said. "See you later!"

Chapter Three

"How's Lottie?" Eva asked Jen as she followed Karl into the surgery.

"She's doing OK," Jen replied. "But it's early days. Your mum thinks we should wait a while longer before putting her up on the website."

Eva frowned. "That doesn't sound good."

"She's been through a lot," Jen reminded her. "Keep your fingers crossed that she'll pull through."

"Hey, we've got an email from Joel!"

Karl announced as he logged on and caught up on the rescue centre messages.

Joel had worked as Heidi's assistant before Jen. Now he was in Russia, working on a big cattle ranch on the frozen prairies.

"What does he say?" Eva asked.

"Happy Christmas and he hopes we all have a great time," Karl reported. "He says he plans to be back in England for New Year."

"Cool!" Eva watched Jen open the flaps of a cardboard box and pick up a pale brown rabbit with floppy ears. "Luckily there's nothing wrong with young Sasha here, except that her ex-owners think she's too much trouble."

Tutting, Eva went to stroke Sasha. She peered into the box. "Who's this?" she asked, gazing at the matching rabbit still in there.

"That's Ruby, Sasha's sister. She's got darker tips to her ears – see."

"Sasha and Ruby," Eva murmured. "What did the owners say?"

"Not much. Just that the family was going away for Christmas and they couldn't find anyone to look after the rabbits. Plus, they've had them for six months and the kids were supposed to groom them and look after them, but they never bothered, so that's how they ended up here."

"Right!" Eva went straight to the computer and found the Animal Magic Newcomers file. "Sasha and Ruby," she typed. "Two fluffy youngsters who need a home together. Are you willing to comb and cuddle them?"

"How does that sound?" she asked Heidi, who had just come in from the kennels.

"Perfect. Karl's already taken their photo. It's very sweet. Before you know it, there'll be a queue of people wanting to adopt them."

"We hope!" Quickly Eva clicked through the list of animals on their website. There was Charlie the lively collie cross and Max the overweight Jack Russell whose owner had gone into hospital. Plus Buffy the pretty black cat with pale grey eyes and Flash the outdoor ginger tom who only came home for tea. On and on the list went. But not many rabbits, Eva noticed, so they stood a good chance of a quick adoption. Then again, perhaps it would be better for Ruby and Sasha not to be adopted before Christmas, she thought. After all, the saying that a dog was for life, not just for Christmas, applied to rabbits, too.

Just then, the door opened and Eva's dad staggered in carrying a tall Christmas tree. "Make way!" he gasped as Eva rushed to hold open the door. "Where do you want this?" he asked Heidi.

"Over by the window, beside the magazine rack," Heidi said, clearing a path.

"Dad chose it and dug it up and put it in a pot especially for us," Mark told her. "He says we're late getting ourselves organized and this is the best one left in the whole garden centre."

"You can smell the pine needles!" Eva loved the build-up to Christmas – fetching the box of decorations from the loft, finding out if the lights still worked, straightening up the silver wings of the fairy that perched on top of the tree. "When can we decorate it?" she asked eagerly.

"After surgery hours," Heidi insisted, as the door opened again and another patient came in – an elderly golden retriever who needed to have some teeth taken out. "Hello, Mr Frears. Bring Penny this way!"

"Busy, busy!" Eva's dad straightened up and eased his back. "It's always like this just before Christmas – people suddenly deciding that they can't cope with their pets."

"Yes, I remember last year," Eva said, standing back to admire the tall, straight tree. She tried not to think too much about careless owners who abandoned their animals, and instead looked ahead to tonight – to trimming the tree and wrapping the presents she'd bought for her mum, dad and Karl. "I love Christmas. It's so cool!" She sighed. "And there's only four days to go!"

Chapter Four

"This time next week it'll all be over," Jen said matter of factly as Eva's dad dropped her off at the train station early next morning. It was three days before Christmas and Jen was travelling home to her family in Ireland for the festive break.

The town was decorated with giant stars, angels and Father Christmases. The streets were crowded with last-minute shoppers.

"I know – is it worth it?" Mark said with a grin. "We all spend too much, eat too much, drink too much ... bah humbug!"

"You old Scrooge!" Eva protested. "I bet you used to love Christmas when you were my age, way back in the olden days!"

"Watch it!" Mark laughed, as he helped Jen with her case. "Have a great time and see you next week."

Jen gave Eva a hug. "Don't forget to drop off those vaccination certificates at Joe Price's place on your way back," she reminded her. "They're in the glovebox. He's arranged for the pups to be collected today, so he needs them in a hurry."

"I won't forget," Eva promised. She waved Jen goodbye as her dad turned his van around. "That means you'll get to meet Mr Price's four gorgeous puppies," she forecast eagerly. "There's Bill and Ben, plus Holly and Ivy. They're all going to be working dogs except Holly."

Over the past twenty-four hours Eva had been too busy to think much about the cute Border collie pups. But now she told her dad all about them as they drove out of town back to Okeham. "Adam Ingleby is going to have Bill. Ben's going to be trained to do sheepdog trials like the ones you see on TV. That's what I'd do if I was allowed to have a collie pup." She said this slowly to make sure her dad paid attention, but she got no response. "They're so clever they can learn any trick you teach them – they can do obstacle courses through plastic tunnels and over fences and little wooden bridges."

"They're definitely top dogs," her dad agreed.

"And Holly is the best of all. She's got the cutest black and white face, with big brown eyes. Her ears kind of fold and flap forward over her face, like someone did origami on them. And her front paws are white with tiny grey speckles—"

"Whoa!" Mark laughed as he took an icy back road up towards Moorview Farm. "I was wondering why you'd left off caring for Lottie and offered to drive into town with me and Jen. Now I know it was because you've fallen seriously in love with one of Joe Price's pups!"

Eva sniffed. "Maybe," she admitted. "But honestly, Dad – Holly is so-o-o cute!"

"How *is* Lottie by the way?" he asked, changing the subject and turning carefully into the lane up to the farm.

"Much better this morning. Mum had to cut some of the knots out of her fur, so she looks a bit scrawny now. But she's a lot stronger. She can stand up while you gently brush her. And she loves being stroked."

"That all sounds good," Mark said, parking his van and leaping out. Eva collected the certificates from the glovebox and followed her dad across the farmyard.

"Hello!" Eva said to a wary grey and white collie who came out of one of the barns to greet them, closely followed by Joe Price.

The dog wagged her bushy tail in response to Eva's voice.

"This is Jess," Mr Price told them. "She's the puppies' mother, and a good old girl. Aren't you, lass? This is her third litter."

"We've just come to drop off the paperwork and the pups' injection cards," Mark explained, handing over the certificates as Eva made a fuss of Jess.

"Can Dad see the puppies?" she asked the farmer, dying to take a peek herself.

"Feel free. They're in the barn, in one of the old cow stalls. You can't miss them."

Eva led her dad into the dark, dusty stone barn, following the sound of lively yapping until they came to a straw-lined stall where Holly, Ivy, Bill and Ben romped and wrestled happily.

"Aren't they gorgeous?" Eva murmured. She picked out the two male puppies –

already bigger and broader than their sisters. Then she pointed to Ivy. "Mr Price is going to keep her," she explained.

"So this one is Holly?" Mark asked, as the fourth pup ran to the door and jumped up as if she were on springs. "Look – she thinks you're here to play."

Eva laughed. "She played hide and seek in Reception yesterday – that was after she'd wrestled with the yard brush!"

"I can see why she's your favourite," her dad admitted. "Look at her cheeky face – you'd swear she's listening to every word we say!"

Just then Mr Price appeared in the doorway. "Mrs Waterson's turned up to collect Holly," he told Eva and Mark. "Can you fetch her, Eva?"

With a deep sigh Eva opened the stall door and slipped inside. Little Holly ran straight over to her and jumped up again. "Hi, Holly. You're coming with me," Eva said quietly. She felt sad as she picked her up. "Say goodbye to your brothers and sister," she whispered.

The puppies yipped and yapped as Eva carried Holly out. "Time to go," she said, sighing again.

"Thank you for calling to tell me that the puppy was ready," Mrs Waterson said to Joe Price out in the farmyard. She spoke so fast it was hard to hear what she was saying. "I'm on my way to drop Lulu off at the kennels and was passing this way."

Still carrying Holly in her arms, Eva paused at the barn door. Mrs Waterson wasn't what she'd pictured. Not that she really knew what she'd been expecting. In the flesh, Holly's new owner was a small, dainty woman in smart trousers and high heels.

"Ah, there you are, Holly!" Mrs Waterson exclaimed, turning towards the barn. "Come here, sweetie. We're going to take you home!"

Who's we? Eva wondered, before spotting a small boy sitting in the large estate car parked beside her dad's van.

Then she noticed that he wasn't alone. Beside him sat a huge, grey Great Dane!

"Todd can't wait to get Holly home," Mrs Waterson told Joe Price. "I promised he could have a puppy as an early Christmas present if he did well in his school exams. Luckily, he got Grade As in most of his subjects, so here we are!"

Eva pursed her lips. "Good for Todd!" she muttered under her breath. "What's the Great Dane called?" she asked out loud.

"That's Lulu. She's really Gina's – Todd's sister's – dog." Mrs Waterson seemed determined to give them the full family history. "Gina has gone with her father to our house in Spain for Christmas, which is why we're putting Lulu in kennels because she's too much of a handful for me and Todd to cope with by ourselves."

Eva wondered why Todd didn't look

very cheerful as he sat in the car, staring out at his new puppy. In fact, he seemed to be definitely *un*-cheerful, sitting beside a dog bigger than he was. The Great Dane seemed equally dejected.

"Todd, come and look!" Mrs Waterson called her son from the car. Todd opened the door and stepped out slowly. He was about eight, with dark hair like his mum's, and wearing jeans and new trainers. "He's not used to the countryside," his mother explained to Joe Price and Eva. "He's a bit nervous around farm animals."

"Remember not to spoil the puppy," Mr Price warned as he gave Mrs Waterson Holly's certificate. "And you too, Todd," he added as, with a nervous smile, the boy took Holly from the farmer. "No treats from the table. No sleeping at the foot of your bed. Otherwise she'll be good for nothing."

"Just like Lulu!" said Mrs Waterson. "I'm always warning Gina that she spoils her!"

The down to earth farmer gave Mrs Waterson a sharp look as if he was having more second thoughts about selling Holly to her. But he was quickly distracted by another car turning into the yard. It was Adam Ingleby from High Trees.

"Happy Christmas, Adam!" Eva's dad called. "Have you come for your pup, too?"

A nod from Adam sent Eva running into the barn to fetch Bill. "Down, Ben. Down, Ivy!" she insisted, reaching for Bill. She closed the stall door and ran back to the yard, clutching the wriggling puppy.

Meanwhile, Mrs Waterson chose that precise moment to fetch her pet carrier

from the car. Lulu seized her chance; she leaped out and broke into a lolloping run towards Todd, jumping up and almost knocking him clean over.

"Watch out, Lulu!" Todd cried as he overbalanced and dropped Holly.

"Lulu, come back!" his mother wailed.

Little Holly rolled clear of Lulu and Todd then raced towards Eva and Bill.

"Yip! Yap!" The excited brother and sister were reunited.

"I couldn't help it!" Todd blurted out before his mum had chance to tell him off.

By this time, Lulu, Bill and Holly were running riot in the yard, with steady old Jess looking on calmly from the barn.

"I'm so sorry about this," Mrs Waterson said in a helpless, exasperated voice. "Oh dear, now I'm going to have a terrible job getting Lulu into the car."

"She's not vicious, is she?" Adam asked, preparing to separate his puppy from Holly and Lulu.

"Not in the least. She wouldn't hurt a fly. But unfortunately my husband is the only one she listens to. I can't get her to do a thing I tell her. Todd, you pick Holly up. If we get her in the car first, maybe Lulu will follow."

Eva watched Todd and Adam rescue their pups and carry them to their cars. Meanwhile, Mark and Joe decided to try and grab hold of Lulu.

"This isn't a game!" Mark exclaimed as Lulu turned to lick his face with her long, slobbery tongue. He took her by the collar and held tight. Slowly but firmly he led the Great Dane to the Watersons' car. "Wow, she's almost as big as Linda's Shetland pony!"

Joe Price shook his head as the mother and son jumped in after Lulu and quickly drove off. "I only hope I've done the right thing," he muttered.

"Well, at least you can trust me – I'll take good care of Bill," Adam promised, pocketing his puppy's certificate and wishing them all Happy Christmas before he drove off.

Eva stood for a long time in the almost empty farmyard. "But honestly, how will Holly cope with having to share a home with Lulu?" she said, though she hardly expected an answer. "And what chance is there of the Watersons taking good care of *her*?"

Chapter Five

"If you were called Eve, not Eva, tomorrow we could all say, 'It's Christmas Eve, Eve'!"

It was two days before Christmas and Eva's grandad, Jimmy Harrison, made his annual family joke. He sat in the kitchen at Animal Magic drinking coffee and eating mince pies.

"Ha-ha, Grandad!" Eva wrinkled her nose. "Isn't it time you made up a new joke? Anyway, come and see the Christmas tree in the surgery. Karl and I decorated it the day before yesterday. It's cool!"

"OK, I'm coming, but mind you don't pull me over!" Her grandfather let himself be tugged by the hand.

Eva crossed the slippery yard with him then opened the door to Reception. Jimmy Harrison stared up at the tree. "Good lord, that's certainly stunning!"

Covered in tiny white lights and draped with silver balls, with the fairy perched precariously on top, the tree took up half the space in the waiting area.

"You chose it for us," Karl reminded his grandad from over at the computer. Then he turned to his mum. "Can I put Lottie up on the website yet?"

"Let's wait till after Christmas," she advised. "She's doing well, but I want to keep her here for at least a week so I can make sure there aren't any complications after her hypothermia. And by the way, Eva, have you checked on Penny this morning?"

Eva nodded. "I went into the kennels before breakfast. She's still a bit tired, but otherwise she seems OK."

"Penny was brought in for dental treatment," Heidi explained to Jimmy.

"But while I was examining her, her owner, Mr Frears, mentioned a bladder problem, and it didn't take me long to diagnose a bladder stone. I operated straight away and removed a stone as big as a peach."

"Ouch!" Karl muttered.

"Poor Penny. It must have really hurt." Glancing over her brother's shoulder, Eva saw that he had booked in an appointment for a Mr and Mrs Jackman to come and see Ruby and Sasha. "What did the Jackmans sound like?" she asked.

"Good. They breed rabbits and are looking for some more flop-eared females. They're coming in this morning at eleven," he reported. "I'm going to spruce the rabbits up a bit. Do you want to help?"

"Listen," Jimmy cut in. "I can see you're

all pretty busy here. Maybe I'll skip the rest of that coffee and come back later."

"No way, Grandad! We're never too busy for you." Eva grabbed him again and led him back across the yard towards the house. "Dad, can you heat up Grandad's coffee?" she yelled. "And if you pour one for Mum I'll take it back out!"

The Jackmans came at eleven and fell in love with Ruby and Sasha. They took them away in a brand-new pet carrier, promising to give the pretty rabbits a fresh start in a loving home. At lunchtime Mr Frears visited Penny and was relieved to see that his faithful girl was well on the road to recovery. Soon afterwards, Karl and Eva took two dogs from the kennels on a walk.

Pixie was a tiny whippet cross who loved to run off the lead, so Eva let her loose. Bruno was the opposite – a burly but timid boxer who stayed close to Karl's side.

As they walked by the river, examining the thin layer of ice at the water's edge and wondering happily about the presents they would soon be opening, Annie ran down the field towards them, waving. "Hey, you two!" she began. "Guess what –

it's going to snow!"

"Says who?" Karl asked, bending down to give Bruno a reassuring pat.

The boxer trembled as Gwinnie cantered down after Annie, her big hooves thudding over the frozen ground. Rosie and Merlin followed more slowly.

"Mum heard it on the weather forecast. It's going to be a white Christmas. And guess what else!"

"Something good?" Eva guessed from her friend's excited expression.

Annie nodded. "Dad's finally finished the stables! Gwinnie, Merlin and Rosie can spend their first night there tonight!"

As if she understood, Gwinnie threw back her head and whinnied.

"Wow, that's cool!" Eva tried not to show that she was sad. "I'll bring their stuff over from our place as soon as I've finished walking Pixie."

"I'll come over and help you," Annie promised. She pulled her red, knitted hat further down her forehead to keep out the biting wind.

"Mum says you can have some special food supplements for Merlin that she's got in the storeroom in the surgery," Eva said. "It's his first winter, so he's bound to feel the cold."

"Thanks, Eva." Annie leaned over the fence, suddenly serious. "I mean, really – thanks for everything you've done for Gwinnie and Merlin – and Rosie!"

Eva gulped back some sudden tears. She was going to miss the horses at Animal Magic! "No problem," she muttered, turning to call Pixie.

"Mum and I will really *really* look after them," Annie promised. "And you can come and see them any time you want!"

"Minus three degrees!" Karl checked the thermometer on the surgery porch.

A starlit night and a frosty morning had passed since the horses had gone to their new stable. It was late afternoon on Christmas Eve and the faint winter sun had already set. Frost sparkled on the roof and the cobbled yard.

Eva stopped sweeping out the empty stables and peered over the door. "Easily cold enough for snow!" she commented hopefully. A white Christmas would be perfect.

The daily jobs at the rescue centre were done – dogs walked, cats fed, small animal cages cleaned – and Heidi was finishing up in the surgery when Eva recognized Adam Ingleby's old red Land

Rover as it pulled up in the yard.

"What does he want at this time on Christmas Eve?" she wondered. "Maybe he ran out of puppy food and the shops all shut early."

"Hi, Adam!" Karl waved. "What's wrong?"

"It's Bill. Is your mother around?" Adam asked, hurriedly carrying his limp and seemingly lifeless puppy towards the surgery.

"I'm here," Heidi assured him, popping her head around the open door, beckoning him inside.

Eva and Karl ran to join them.

"There's something wrong with Bill," Adam told Heidi. "The first thing I noticed was last night – he was off his food. I didn't think too much of it at first – I put it down to a delayed reaction to his vaccinations; then this morning I noticed he had the sniffles."

"Let's take a look," Heidi said, carrying Bill into the examination room. She felt his stomach and peered into his mouth, then took his temperature.

"Not good, is it?" Adam guessed.

"His temperature's sky-high," Heidi answered, frowning when the puppy's sides heaved and he let out a dry, hacking cough. "His lungs sound pretty congested, too." She checked his chest with the stethoscope.

"Well?" Adam prompted.

Eva and Karl watched anxiously. They could tell by the look on their mother's face that she was worried.

"Bill's got the symptoms of something quite serious," she told Adam. "It wouldn't be covered by his first set of injections for the parvo virus and so on. No – this is quite different."

"What is it?" Adam wanted the diagnosis, but Heidi wouldn't be rushed.

"The question is, where would Bill have picked it up?" she wondered. "If it is what I'm thinking, it would be highly infectious. But if it was at Joe Price's place ... surely Joe would have let me know!"

"What is it, Mum?" Eva asked, suddenly afraid for poor little Bill. The grey and white speckled puppy lay on his side on the blue disinfected surface, hardly responding to her mum's thorough examination.

"I'm not totally sure." Heidi still wouldn't commit herself. She thought some more then looked straight at Adam and made her diagnosis. "I think it *might* be kennel cough," she admitted at last. "And if it is, I'm afraid it's very bad news indeed."

Chapter Six

"Otherwise known as Canine Infectious Trach-eo-bronch-itis." Karl went over to the computer and Googled kennel cough. He read out his findings to Eva while Heidi discussed Bill's treatment with Adam.

"Canine Infectious Trach...?" Eva echoed doubtfully, then tailed off.

"Coughing localised to the windpipe and lungs. A respiratory disease caused by several different viruses or bacteria."

"It sounds horrible!" Eva exclaimed. "Maybe we should flag up a warning on the website? You know – 'Watch out for kennel cough!' – so everyone realizes it's going round. How do dogs catch it?"

"They can pick it up in any number of places," Heidi broke in as she came out of the examination room carrying Bill. "Dog shows, training classes, kennels – hence its common name, kennel cough. But in fact, they can catch it just by being taken for a walk in an area where another infected dog has been – like a park, or a field. It's often impossible to track down the original culprit."

"But you think you can cure him?" Adam asked anxiously.

Heidi nodded and unlocked the drugs cabinet. "I hope he'll respond to these antibiotics. I'll also give you a spray which will open up his bronchial passages and help him to breathe more easily."

"Don't we have to keep him in overnight?" Eva asked.

"No, but Adam, you should keep Bill in complete isolation and change his bedding daily. Make sure the room where you keep him is well ventilated. And call me if you're worried."

"Even on Christmas Day?" the young farmer checked.

"In this job we never close!" Heidi smiled as she opened the door and handed Bill over to his owner. "Happy Christmas!" she called to Adam. "And try not to be too concerned!"

"So where on earth did Bill pick up his infection?" Eva asked anxiously. "I'm sure he never even left Mr Price's farm before yesterday, except to come here for his vaccinations!"

Heidi shook her head. "It's a mystery. Like I said, I'm certain Joe would have called me if any dog on his farm had contracted the virus. And he'd have known to keep the animal in strict isolation. This thing can last up to three months and it's very infectious. Most kennels won't take a dog in unless it's been vaccinated against kennel cough."

"And what happens if you don't treat it?"

Karl wanted to know.

"There are all sorts of complications – permanent lung damage for instance. And that can be life threatening."

"You mean, Bill could die?" Eva asked.

"It's possible. But we've diagnosed it early and he's getting treatment. It's the dogs who never see a vet who suffer most."

"So we ought to ring Mr Price and tell him about Bill right now," Karl suggested.

"Definitely." Heidi picked up the phone and dialled the number of Moorview Farm. "Hello, Joe? It's Heidi Harrison here..."

"And we'll have to ring Mrs Waterson," Eva remembered. "Mum, ask Mr Price for Mrs Waterson's address and phone number. We need to find out if Holly has caught the virus."

Heidi nodded. "…Yes, Joe, that's right. Yes, I'm 95% sure it's kennel cough. Do me a favour and check Jess and the remaining puppies… And can you give me the number for the people who bought Holly? …Oh, I see – yes, that's a problem… No, leave it with me. Call me if you want me to come out and check on Jess, Ben and Ivy – any time of day or night. OK, yes, thanks."

"What's happened?" Eva asked as Heidi put down the phone. She could tell from her mum's face that something was wrong.

"Joe doesn't have Mrs Waterson's details anymore. Once she'd picked up Holly he threw them away. He knows they came from 'town', but isn't even sure which one."

"That's bad news," Karl muttered, closing down the computer. "Now what are we going to do?"

Frantically Eva thought back to the scene in Joe Price's yard. She remembered how she'd run into the barn to collect first Holly and then Bill, leaving the other two pups safe in the cow stall. Then she recalled how Mrs Waterson had opened her car door and let Lulu jump out and lollop all over the yard. "Mrs Waterson said she couldn't get Lulu to do a thing she told her," she muttered to herself.

"What's that?" Karl asked.

"I said, Mrs Waterson admitted that she had no control over Lulu, her Great Dane." It all came flooding back to Eva. "That was the reason she was on her way to take Lulu to the kennels for Christmas."

"Well remembered, Eva!" Karl quickly saw how this would help. "Did she say which kennels?"

Eva shook her head. "But it must be somewhere nearby because she said she was passing Moorview Farm on the way there, and there can't be that many boarding kennels around!"

"Here's a list," Heidi said, taking a piece of card out of a desk drawer. "Nesfield Boarding Kennels and Okeham Cattery and Kennels are the most likely. Try them first then go on down the list. A Great Dane named Lulu shouldn't be too hard to track down!"

"Nesfield is a 'no'," Karl reported after the first quick call. Time was ticking by. Before long the offices at all the kennels would be closed and wouldn't open again until after Boxing Day.

"Okeham said no, too," Eva reported from the other telephone. "They said they didn't have any Watersons on their books, and no Great Danes either."

"OK, I'll try Ghyll Bank," Karl decided, picking up the phone again.

Eva's heart was starting to sink. "Hello, is that Low Lane Kennels?" she asked after she'd dialled a second number.

"Yes, but I'm afraid we're fully booked," the man's voice replied. "We did have one last-minute vacancy, but that's been filled this afternoon."

"No, it's OK, I don't want to board my dog," Eva said quickly. "I'm phoning from Animal Magic Rescue Centre, trying to track down a Great Dane. I was wondering – do you have one called Lulu boarding with you?"

There was a pause before the voice replied. "That rings a bell. Let me check with my wife."

Eva held her breath and waited.

"Yes, I thought so." The man at Low Lane came back to the phone. "That's how our last-minute vacancy came up – a family named Waterson had booked their dog in over the phone. But when they turned up here they had no vaccination certificates. The lady owner said she'd been too busy to get it done. And, of course, we don't take a dog unless the owner can produce the right paperwork.

Anyway, I noticed the dog already had a watery discharge from her nose, plus a bit of a cough."

"So what happened?" Eva asked, hanging on the man's every word.

"We turned them away."

"So Mrs Waterson took Lulu home?"

"That's right. To be honest, the dog looked like a bit of a handful. I didn't envy the little Border collie pup she had with her."

Eva's heart rate quickened as she asked the kennel owner one last question. "Please can you give me the Watersons' address and telephone number?"

There was another long pause before the man replied. "Sorry," he reported back. "My wife wiped their details off the computer."

Chapter Seven

"Look – it's snowing!" Eva's dad told her after tea. He led her to the kitchen window and made her look outside. "It's like a real life Christmas card!"

Eva watched big white flakes float down from the dark sky. Already the yard and the rescue centre roof were covered in a thick layer of snow.

"Why the glum face on Christmas Eve?" Mark asked gently. "Do you want to tell me what's up?"

"No thanks, Dad. I'm OK."

"No you're not," he insisted, drawing her towards the log fire. Heidi and Karl were in the living room, stacking presents under the house Christmas tree. "Come on – spill the beans!"

"I can't help worrying about Holly," Eva confessed. Once she'd started, the whole story tumbled out. "Puppies can die from kennel cough," she ended up breathlessly. "And you know something – I bet Todd Waterson and his mum won't know what to do if Holly gets sick!"

"You can't say that for sure," Mark warned. "Listen, Eva, I know this is hard for you, but it may be something we can't do anything about. Without knowing which town the Watersons live in, we might just have to let the problem go."

Eva's eyes filled with tears. "But this is

their fault. I'm sure Lulu is the one who's infecting the others – the man at Low Lane Kennels said she had a runny nose and a bad cough."

Mark sighed. "We still can't help, however much we might want to."

Eva nodded as a tear splashed on to her cheek.

"So we just have to accept that Holly and Lulu have disappeared and concentrate on enjoying Christmas, OK?"

This time Eva couldn't even manage a nod. Instead, she sniffed, then said, "I'm going out to check the cattery and say hi to Lottie."

"Good idea," her dad agreed. "Put your puffa jacket on. It's cold out there."

Eva found the allotment cat curled up and asleep in her warm bed. "You look snug," she whispered.

At the sound of Eva's voice, Lottie opened her eyes.

"Sorry, I didn't mean to wake you!" Eva leaned into the unit and stroked the thin cat. "Look at your fur – it's all spiky and uneven."

Miaow! Lottie stood up and brushed against Eva's hand for another stroke.

"There! You're so cute. How did you end

up under an allotment shed?"

Miaow! Lottie said again.

"Never mind, after Christmas we're going to find you a lovely home with a nice kind person to take really good care of you," Eva promised.

Nearby other cats miaowed for attention so Eva went down the row stroking them and talking gently. Then, after ten minutes, she decided it was time to go back to the house. "I'll try to be more cheerful!" she promised Lottie as she took one last look. "After all, it's not fair to ruin everyone's Christmas, is it?"

Miaow! Lottie replied, settling down to sleep again.

Eva left the cattery and quietly closed the door. She turned up the collar of her jacket and stepped out into the snowy yard. Further along Main Street she heard the sound of carol singers.

"Good King Wenceslas looked out

On the Feast of Stephen..."

Eva walked across the yard, gazing up at the whirling, ice-cold flakes. Suddenly she heard footsteps round the front of the house. "Who's that?" she wondered.

Perhaps it was one of the carol singers running ahead of the others to knock on doors. She went round the side to take a look, but there was no one there.

"That's funny," Eva muttered, spotting scuff marks and footprints in the snow. The footsteps headed to and from the front doorstep. "Weird."

She looked up and down the street – no,

definitely no one there. Then she turned and stopped dead.

There was a small, dark shape on the doorstep. Eva stepped closer to take a look.

The shape moved – a small creature, half covered in snow. She looked again.

"Yip!" the tiny thing cried.

At first Eva couldn't believe what she was seeing. A black and white puppy with speckled front legs was shivering and crying on the doorstep.

"Holly?" Eva whispered.

The collie pup gave another tiny bark.

"Oh, Holly!" Eva gasped, picking her up and knocking frantically on her own front door. "Mum, Dad, Karl, open the door quick! It's Holly – she's been abandoned on our doorstep. Quick, before she freezes to death!"

"I'll keep her warm by the fire while you run for the medicine and equipment you need," Mark said to Heidi.

Karl had opened the door and let Eva and Holly in, then the whole family sprang into action. "Yes, we mustn't take her anywhere near the other dogs," Heidi agreed. "She probably has kennel cough, just like Bill. We'll have to isolate her until the infection is dealt with."

Heidi ran across to the surgery while Eva gave her dad a towel to dry the melting snow from a still-shivering Holly.

"I'm going out to look for the person who dumped her," Karl decided, grabbing his jacket. He left by the front door and ran up Main Street.

"Maybe she found her own way here," Eva's dad suggested after Karl had left.

But Eva shook her head. "I heard footsteps. There were tracks in the snow." She stood to one side as her mum dashed back in and got to work.

"The same symptoms as Bill's," Heidi muttered once she'd listened to Holly's chest. "And this time there's a discharge from her eyes."

Eva's heart beat fast, but she tried not to panic. "Don't worry, Holly," she whispered, crouching down to stroke her favourite puppy. "Mum knows what she's doing. She's a really good vet!"

Poor Holly gazed up at Eva with a scared look in her dark-brown eyes.

Eva stroked her gently. "Now that you're here at Animal Magic, you'll be safe. I won't leave you until you're better, cross my heart!"

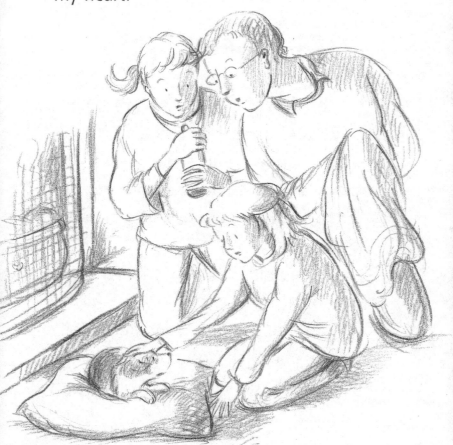

Chapter Eight

"It's a total mystery," Karl reported. He'd been up and down Main Street, quizzing the carol singers and other passers-by. "Nobody saw anything unusual – no cars pulling up outside our house, no strangers – nothing!"

"Just dumped!" Eva said angrily. "How cruel is that!"

"Sshh." Heidi had finished treating Holly and now appealed for everyone to be calm. "What's done is done. The main thing is that she is receiving good care."

"Poor Holly," Eva sighed, afraid to pick her up yet longing to cuddle her. The puppy lay on a big cushion, soaking up the heat from the log fire.

Holly took a short breath then let out a noisy dry cough. She coughed for so long that Eva was scared she had something stuck in her throat.

"She sounds awful," Karl muttered.

"Hmm, but the antibiotics will soon kick in," Heidi told them. "And I'm thinking an old-fashioned remedy might help, too."

"What is it?" Eva said eagerly. She would do anything to help Holly.

"Bring her upstairs. We'll run a hot bath and close the bathroom door. We'll keep Holly in there for twenty minutes so she can inhale the steam. That'll ease the cough."

"Like a sauna," Karl realized as Eva carried the puppy upstairs.

"I'll sit with her," Eva offered.

And so all through the rest of Christmas Eve, Eva kept her promise not to leave Holly on her own – first of all in the steam-filled bathroom, then down in the kitchen again, settling her back on her comfy cushion and gently patting the tiny puppy's chest as her mum had showed her.

"That's called coupage," Heidi explained. "It's another way of helping the cough."

"I think it's working," Karl said. "She seems better already."

By bedtime, Eva had made a decision. "I'm not going to bed tonight," she announced. "I'll stay down here and sleep in a sleeping bag next to Holly."

Her dad smiled. "Don't forget to bring your Christmas stocking down with you. And I'd better let Father Christmas know that you're kipping downstairs!"

"Da-ad!" Eva tutted.

"It's OK, I'll fetch your sleeping bag and pyjamas." Her mum laughed. "And we'll find the blow-up mattress for you. Come on, let's get organized. It's late and I don't know about anyone else, but I'm exhausted."

Fifteen minutes later, Eva snuggled down in her sleeping bag beside Holly, making sure she could see her in the dim light of the dying fire. "Don't worry," she whispered as her mum checked the fireguard, turned off the light and closed the door. "Everything's going to be all right – I promise!"

Outside the snow kept on falling. By midnight the whole of Okeham was sparkling and silent. Then the sky cleared. Stars shone and dawn crept in with a faint, pink light.

Eva woke to the sound of Holly whimpering. "What is it?" she whispered, wondering at first where she was, then realizing she was on a mattress on the kitchen floor. The empty Christmas stocking which her dad had hung from the back of a chair was now stuffed with brightly-wrapped presents.

The little puppy sat up on her cushion, ears pricked. She gave a sharp yap.

"It's OK, I'm still here," Eva whispered, surprised that she'd managed to sleep at all. The last thing she remembered was drowsily gazing at Holly, who was asleep on her cushion. Now it was almost light – it was Christmas Day!

Holly barked again.

"Sshh!"

"Yip! Yap!" The puppy slid off her cushion and ran to the door.

"Hey, you must really be feeling better!" Eva exclaimed. "But what's bothering you?" Sleepily, Eva struggled out of her sleeping bag and followed Holly. She peered through the window at the snowy yard. "Oh!" she gasped, frozen to the spot with shock.

A small, worried face was peering back at her. The face was full of fear as its eyes met Eva's.

"Todd?"

In an instant the face had vanished. Eva hurriedly unlocked the door. She ran out in her bare feet, just in time to see Todd Waterson sprinting away.

"Please let me follow him!" Eva begged. She was back in the kitchen, shoving her feet into her wellies and flinging her jacket on over her pyjamas. "Mum, I have to go!"

Heidi had heard the kitchen door open and come downstairs to investigate. "Follow who? Eva, hang on a minute – tell me exactly what happened!"

"Todd Waterson – he was here a few seconds ago, peeping through the window!"

"Are you sure you weren't dreaming?"

"No, Holly heard him creeping around outside. She started to bark. That's how come I woke up." Seconds were slipping by. Todd was getting clean away.

"But what was he doing here at this time in the morning? How did he get here?" To Heidi none of this made sense. She stood in front of the door, blocking Eva's way out.

"All I know is – he was here!"

"What's going on?" Karl mumbled, appearing at the foot of the stairs, his hair messed up, his face still bleary with sleep.

"Karl, get dressed!" Eva cried. "You have to help me find Todd. He's just been here, obviously looking for Holly."

"You mean, he's the one who dumped her?" Karl asked.

Eva nodded. "How else would he know she was here?"

"Happy Christmas, everyone." It was Mark's turn to interrupt. He'd followed Karl downstairs, still half asleep. "Is it time to open presents?"

"Happy Christmas, Dad," Eva gabbled. She was desperate to follow Todd, but her hopes of finding him were fading. "Karl, hurry up – Todd's getting away!"

"Eva says she saw Todd Waterson snooping around the house," Heidi explained to Mark. "I know, I'm surprised, too. But I suppose we have to let Karl and Eva take a look."

Mark nodded.

"Hurray!" *At last!* Eva hurried across to Holly to explain. "We won't be long. You have to wait here where it's nice and warm. Mum says you have to rest as much as possible!"

Holly wagged her little tail.

"Stay!" Eva held up a warning finger. "I'll see you in a bit – OK!"

Chapter Nine

"So which way did Todd go?" Karl wondered as he and Eva stepped out into the first light of Christmas Day.

"That's easy – he went past Annie's house!" Eva pointed to one set of clear footprints – the only ones to spoil the smooth covering of snow.

"Let's go!" Karl cried. "If we hurry we can catch him up."

"He looked pretty scared when he saw

me," Eva said. "He'll be running away as fast as he can."

"Look here – a skid mark – he must have slipped."

"And here's another one." Eva pointed to where Todd's footprints turned down a side street and headed downhill. Her own feet crunched into the crisp snow. "Whoo!" she cried, grabbing on to a gatepost as she slid and almost fell.

"The trail is leading us to Riverview Road," Karl pointed out. "I wonder who Todd Waterson knows down here?"

Eva shrugged. It was weird being out so early, when all her friends would be jumping out of warm beds and tearing at wrapping paper to see what Father Christmas had brought. "Let's go and find out," she said, following Todd's tracks to the short row of terraced houses overlooking the river. The trail led into the garden of number four.

"Are we going to knock at the door?" Karl asked. "Won't it look a bit – weird?"

"Who cares?" Eva replied. "All that matters is finding out why Todd dumped Holly on our doorstep!"

She knocked loudly on the red door and waited.

After a while there was the sound of someone unlatching the lock, and a woman's head appeared. "Yes?" she asked warily. She was in her dressing gown, with white towelling slippers on her feet.

"Sorry to bother you," Eva said, trying to peer down the hallway. "We're looking for Todd Waterson."

"He's in bed," the woman answered. "Anyway – have you any idea what time it is?"

Just then, a second woman appeared in the corridor. Eva recognized her right away as Todd's mother. "We definitely got the right place!" she muttered to Karl, who was hanging back and looking embarrassed. "Mrs Waterson, we need to speak to Todd!"

"As my sister said, Todd's still asleep," Mrs Waterson insisted. "What's this all about?"

"Are you sure he's in bed?" Eva held her ground. "I think you'd better check."

"Look here!" Mrs Waterson stepped out into the porch. "I've seen you before – up at Moorview Farm."

Eva nodded. "My mum and dad run Animal Magic Rescue Centre. Mum did Holly's vaccinations."

"So you're here to check up on Holly when you should be at home with your family, enjoying Christmas like everyone else. I think I'd better speak to your parents."

"I'm going to check on Todd," her sister decided, then disappeared upstairs.

"If you must know, I left Lulu and Holly at home," Andrea Waterson told Eva with a hostile stare. "A neighbour is popping in on them while we're away."

"But you can't do that, even if it was

true!" Eva cried. "Holly has only been with you a couple of days. She's just a puppy. It's not fair to leave her alone like that!"

"But it's *not* true." Karl stepped forward with the facts. "Because we've got Holly at Animal Magic."

"That's not possible!" Mrs Waterson gasped.

Her sister ran downstairs in a panic. "Andrea, Todd isn't in his bed!"

Mrs Waterson's hands flew to her face.

"It's been slept in, but he isn't there now!" Todd's aunt confirmed. She looked hard at Eva. "Tell us what's going on!"

"That's what we're trying to find out!" Eva muttered. "Todd was at our place just a few minutes ago, peering in through the window – we followed his trail back here."

"It's obvious he snuck out," Karl said thoughtfully as Andrea Waterson and her sister started to panic. "And the tracks show that he definitely came back. I reckon he's hiding somewhere close by because he's scared…"

"Scared of what?" Mrs Waterson interrupted. "Oh, this is terrible!"

"Wait a second!" Eva's sharp eyes had spotted a trail of water across the hallway tiles. It led to a cupboard under the stairs. "That could be melted snow from Todd's boots."

In an instant Andrea Waterson had dashed down the hall and flung open the low door. "Oh, Todd – there you are!" she cried, dragging him out. "Oh, poor boy – you're shivering. What on earth have you been doing?"

Eva and Karl sat at Todd's aunt's kitchen table, waiting for him to explain everything. Todd was crying, even though his mum had hugged him and told him over and over that he wasn't in trouble, whatever he'd done. "But you have to tell us what happened," she insisted gently. "How did Holly arrive on Karl and Eva's doorstep?"

"You won't be cross with me?" Todd whispered nervously.

His mum held his hand and shook her head. "Of course not."

"OK. I did it because Holly was poorly," Todd confessed.

"Did what?" His Aunt Fiona made everyone a mug of hot chocolate then sat down at the table to listen.

"I smuggled Holly out of our house in a big bag of Christmas presents – because she wasn't very well and I didn't want to leave her all alone."

"Holly would have been perfectly OK with Mrs Browning looking after her..." Mrs Waterson began. Then she blushed and fell silent.

"You didn't even realize that Lulu was poorly," Todd went on. "I tried to tell you, but you were too busy to listen."

"So then what happened?" Eva prompted. "After you smuggled Holly out in the bag of presents, what then?"

"Mum drove here to Aunt Fiona's and I sneaked Holly upstairs. But she was really poorly now – coughing and being sick – and I was scared."

"So you snuck out and brought her to Animal Magic," Karl concluded.

Todd nodded. "I'd seen the sign outside the rescue centre when we drove past. I left Holly on the doorstep because I needed you to look after her."

"It would've been better to knock on the door," Eva told him. "As it was, it was lucky we found her."

Todd hung his head. "I was going to, then I heard you walking across the yard and I was scared. Really scared. So I ran away. Is Holly OK?" he asked, wiping tears from his face with the back of his hand. "Is she getting better?"

"Slowly," Eva told him. "She's got kennel cough. Mum's given her some medicine, but it'll take a while for Holly to get completely better."

"But you definitely did the right thing, Todd," Karl added. "If you hadn't brought her to Animal Magic she might have died."

At this, Andrea Waterson sprang to her own defence. "I couldn't bring the dogs here, could I?" she appealed to her sister. "There isn't room for Lulu in this tiny house. Besides, it was only for a couple of days."

"And you didn't realize they were sick." Fiona tried to help, but it only seemed to make her sister feel worse. She turned to Eva. "What about Lulu?" she asked quietly. "Does she have this kennel cough, too?"

"We think she's the one who had it first, and she passed it on to Holly and Bill," Eva replied before turning to her brother. "Karl, what are we going to do about Lulu?"

"We'll tell Mum," he decided quickly. "Mrs Waterson, will you lend us your house key? Dad will be able to drive over and bring Lulu back to the rescue centre. But if we're going to help Lulu, we have to do it now – before presents, or breakfast, or anything!"

Chapter Ten

"See how well Holly's doing," Eva said as she led Todd into the kitchen at Animal Magic. "She's almost back to normal!"

The puppy stood up and wagged her tail.

Todd heaved a sigh of relief. "Hi, Holly. It's me!" He turned to Eva. "Can I pick her up?"

She nodded. Through the open door she could hear Mrs Waterson talking to her mum.

"You can cuddle her, but don't let her get too excited," Eva warned Todd before she tuned in to the conversation in the living room.

"Mark and Karl shouldn't be too long, snow permitting," Heidi was saying to Todd's mum. "The sooner they get back here with Lulu the better. If she's already had this infection for a number of days, there may be secondary problems which need to be looked at as soon as possible."

"I see now that I've been terribly irresponsible," Mrs Waterson said after a long pause. "But the truth is – I've been very busy trying to organize Christmas without my husband."

"That's OK," Heidi said kindly. "You don't have to explain."

"I'm sorry I've made such a mess of looking after the dogs."

Heidi nodded. "Like we always say – people must think long and hard about having pets if they're going to feel tied down by them over holiday periods."

"I'm afraid that's true for us – given that we own the house in Spain. I didn't really think things through when I gave way to Gina's pressure for us to have a dog. As for buying Holly for Todd – it was more my idea than his. I thought he'd like to have a puppy and be the same as his sister."

"Listen, I can hear Mark's van in the yard." Heidi cut the conversation short. "If you'll excuse me...!"

Hearing this, Eva peered through the window. "Here comes Dad!" she told Todd, leaving Holly with him and his mum and dashing outside. "Have you got Lulu?" she asked Karl, who jumped out of the van first.

He nodded. "She's in a bad way – she's gone downhill really fast since last night when the neighbour went in to feed her."

"That's what happens with this illness," Heidi said. She reminded Mark and Karl to keep Lulu away from the kennels as they lifted the sick Great Dane out of the van. "Best to carry her into the empty stable block. We'll keep her isolated and make a bed for her there."

Quickly the arrangements were made. While Heidi went to fetch antibiotics and a saline drip, Eva ran ahead into the stables to arrange a bed of straw covered by a clean horse blanket from the tack room. Mark and Karl laid her down gently.

"She's wheezing badly," Mark warned Heidi when she came back. "And she's hardly got the energy to stand, let alone walk."

Nodding, Heidi began her treatment. "The problem here is that there's an organism called mycoplasma involved – a hybrid of both a virus and a bacterium – which means that the antibiotic isn't foolproof."

Once more Eva was caught by a sudden rush of worry. She knelt down by Lulu and stroked her softly.

The Great Dane slowly raised her head and nuzzled Eva's hand.

"Let's hope Lulu's immune system is strong enough to kick in and fight back," Heidi said, standing back at last. She and Mark made way for Todd and his mother, who had just come into the stable to see Lulu.

They all gazed down at the patient.

"How is she?" Mrs Waterson asked.

"She's doing OK," Heidi replied. "You can stay with her for a while if you like."

Todd nodded. He knelt in the straw and stroked Lulu.

"We'll be in the kitchen if you need us," Mark assured the Watersons, leading Heidi, Karl and Eva out of the stable and closing the door.

Back in the house, Eva grew thoughtful. "Mum, if Holly and Lulu do get better, will they have to go back to the Watersons?"

"Yes, wouldn't it be better if we put the dogs on our website and found new owners who could look after them properly?" Karl argued eagerly.

Heidi glanced out across the snowy yard. "Lulu and Holly haven't been signed over to us," she pointed out.

Mark agreed. "At Animal Magic we can't take in pets without their owners' permission."

"True," Karl admitted.

Eva wasn't convinced. All she could think about was Lulu and adorable Holly. "But the Watersons aren't very good with animals. Holly's been through a lot already – I'd hate to think what else could go wrong!"

"Let's talk about it later," Heidi warned as she looked out of the window and saw Todd and his mum appear at the stable door.

Eva sighed loudly.

"At least we can give Mrs Waterson the name of a good dog trainer," her dad suggested. "Then, when Lulu and Holly get better, we'll know they have access to the best possible teacher."

"Hmm," Heidi said slowly. She seemed

to be deep in thought.

"I reckon Mrs Waterson will agree to do that," Karl said. "She seems pretty sorry about what happened."

Heidi patted Eva's arm as the Watersons walked across the yard towards the house. "Mark, let's have a quick word," she suggested. "Wait here," she told Eva and Karl, swiftly taking their dad outside.

"What's going on?" Eva wondered.

Karl listened at the door. "I can't hear a word," he told her, going to the window instead. "All I can tell you is that Mum and Dad have finished talking and decided to intercept the Watersons!"

"I'm still worried, Karl. I wish we could wave a magic wand and change the Watersons into perfect dog owners!"

"If only!" he sighed.

Together they watched their mum and

dad having a long talk with Mrs Waterson.
Todd listened quietly, nodding whenever
his mum turned to ask him a question. He
waited patiently as she took out her
mobile phone and made a long call. Then
at last, Todd and his mother walked with
Heidi and Mark towards the house.

"Karl and Eva, Todd has something to
say to you," Mrs Waterson announced as
all four came into the kitchen.

Eva held Holly safe in her arms, feeling her rough pink tongue lick her fingers.

"Thank you for saving Holly," Todd began.

"And thank you!" Eva said softly. "Bringing her here to Okeham with you was what really saved her life."

Todd swallowed hard. "Your mum and dad and my mum have been talking about Holly and Lulu," he went on. "Mum's decided that it would be best to put Lulu on the Animal Magic website."

"You mean – you want us to find her a new home?" Eva gasped. She guessed that Todd was bravely holding back the tears. "And do you think so, too?"

He nodded. "We called Dad and Gina and they agreed that we weren't looking after Lulu very well."

"She needs a house with a bigger

garden and someone who can take her for long walks," Mrs Waterson explained.

"When she gets better, can you find her somewhere like that?" Todd asked Eva and Karl.

"You bet!" Karl said quickly, while Eva stared at Todd in surprise. "Ssshh, stay still, Holly!" she murmured, as the puppy wriggled on her lap.

"And what else, Todd?" his mother prompted.

"We haven't looked after Holly very well either," he said miserably. "She was having a lovely time with her brothers and sister at Moorview Farm, and ever since she came to our house she's been sad."

"Wait! What are you saying?" Eva gasped. She glanced at her mum and dad, who had on their secretive, "Don't ask us!" expressions.

"Do you mean you want us to find a new home for Holly too?" Karl asked excitedly. "A home in the country, where she has space to run around and herd sheep and do proper sheepdog things?"

There was a long pause while Eva held tightly to precious Holly.

"Not exactly," Todd said with a frown.

"What then?" Eva asked, leaping up.

Todd came to stand close to her and the puppy. "We'd like you to keep Holly," he murmured.

"Me?" Eva said faintly.

"You and Karl," her dad said, watching her face slowly light up. "Your mum and I talked it through and we both agreed to break our golden rule of no family pets."

"Just this once!" Heidi warned. "Since you're so fond of Holly and this is a very special case."

Eva went over to Karl. "Did you hear that?" she said, excitedly.

Karl took the puppy in his arms. He nodded.

"Karl's too happy to speak!" Mark laughed. "So, what about you, Eva? Do you think it's a good idea?"

"Pinch me, somebody, and tell me it's true!" she cried. She beamed at Todd. "Don't worry – Holly will live here with us and you can come and see her whenever you want!"

"How about straight after Christmas

dinner?" Mark suggested with a wink.

Todd nodded eagerly. He watched Karl set Holly down on her cushion by the fire then looked out across the yard, past the stables to the fields beyond. "She's going to love it here, isn't she, Mum?"

"Definitely," Mrs Waterson agreed. Then quietly she took Todd's hand and led him towards the car.

"This is the *best* Christmas ever!" Eva cried.

The turkey was roasting in the oven, the presents were opened and wrapping paper lay scattered over the kitchen floor.

Karl laughed as Holly got tangled up in red ribbon, then pounced on Eva's chocolate orange.

"Happy Christmas, everyone!" their grandad called as he opened the door and kicked off his snowy boots. There was an inviting smell of Christmas dinner, newly opened parcels ... and chaos in the kitchen. "Good heavens, what's going on here?"

Eva flew to greet him. "Grandad, guess what's happened!"

"Has Father Christmas paid you a visit?" he asked with a twinkle in his eye.

"Better than that," Karl said, a grin spreading from ear to ear.

From under a large piece of silver wrapping, Holly made a sudden pounce at their grandad's feet. She growled and crouched down, ready to attack his thick, grey socks.

"Mum and Dad have broken their rule!" Eva cried, swooping to pick Holly up and cuddle her. She and Karl had a puppy of their very own – it was a dream come true. "Holly is going to live at Animal Magic. She's ours – to keep!"

Collect all the books in the series!

Honey
The unwanted puppy

Charlie
The home-alone kitten

Merlin
The homeless foal

Rusty
The injured fox cub

Bella
The runaway rabbit

Dilly
The lost duckling

Harry
The abandoned hamster

Barney
The baby hedgehog

Holly
The doorstep puppy

Visit the Animal Magic website:
www.animalmagicrescue.net

And look out for Animal Rescue's next title!

Rosie

The problem pony

When Eva's next-door neighbour, Linda Brooks, slips on ice and breaks her leg, she's unable to look after Rosie, the Shetland pony and Animal Magic soon has her back on its books. Can Eva and Karl find a perfect new home for the picky little pony ... and one that's close enough to visit!